Little Wolf's
Haunted Hall
for
Small Horrors

First American edition published in 2000
by Carolrhoda Books, Inc.

Published by arrangement with HarperCollins Publishers Ltd, London,
England. Originally published under the title LITTLE WOLF'S
HAUNTED HALL FORSMALL HORRORS.

Carolrhoda Books, Inc., a division of Lerner Publishing Group
241 First Avenue North, Minneapolis, MN 55401 U.S.A.

Website address: www.lernerbooks.com

Library of Congress Cataloging-in-Publication Data

Whybrow, Ian.
Little Wolf's haunted hall for small horrors / Ian Whybrow ; illustrated
by Tony Ross.—American ed.
p. cm.
Summary: In a series of letters to his parents, Little Wolf describes his
attempts to create "the scariest school in the world" and convince his
ghostly Uncle Bigbad to teach a magic class.
ISBN 1-57505-412-4 (lib. bdg. : alk. paper)
[1. Schools—Fiction. 2. Animals—Fiction. 3. Uncles—Fiction. 4.
Ghosts—Fiction. 5. Letters—Fiction.] I. Ross, Tony, ill. II. Title.

PZ7.W6225 Lm 2000
[Fic]—dc21   00-025290

Manufactured in the United States of America
2 3 4 5 6 7 – BP – 06 05 04 03 02 01

Little Wolf's
Haunted Hall
for
Small Horrors

Ian Whybrow
Illustrated by Tony Ross

Carolrhoda Books, Inc., Minneapolis

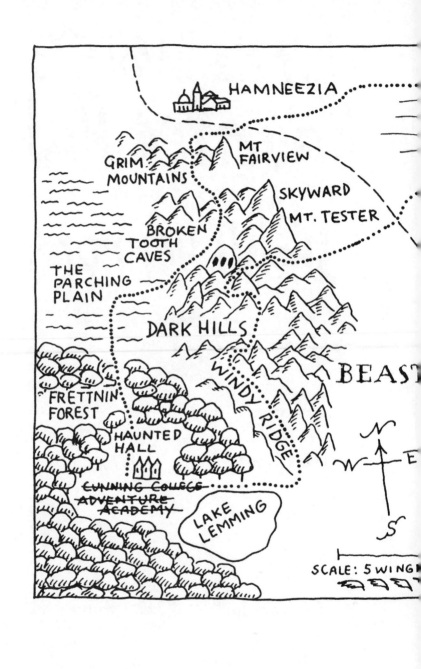

THE BEST SCHOOL
FOR BRUTE BEASTS

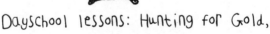

HUNTING AND HAUNTING OUR SPECIALITY

Heads: L. W. Wolf and Yeller Wolf
Caretaker and Fixy Boy: Stubbs Crow
Small Horror: Smellybreff Wolf
School Spirit and Spook: Mister Bigbad Wolf, R.I.P.

Dayschool lessons: Hunting for Gold,
Spooksuit making, Flying, etc.
Nightschool lessons: Walking through Walls,
Shocking for Beginners and All That
Playtime: Hello Ween and Midnight Feasts

HAUNTED HALL
FOR SMALL HORRORS

Dear Mom and Dad,

Please please PLEEEEZ don't be so grrrish. It's not fair Dad keeps saying, "GET A MOVE ON, LAZYBONES. OPEN YOUR SCHOOL QUICK." Just because he has a fangache, I bet. Boo, shame. Today I will do the news 1st, then draw cheery pics for him after.

Yeller and Stubbs and me are trying and trying. Paws crossed we open soonly. But did you forget our 1 big problem I told you about? I will tell you wunce more. It is the ghost of Uncle Bigbad. He is fine, in a dead way, but he keeps being nasty. He says, "Do this and do that, or no more haunting from me." Just because he knows we *neeeed* him for our School Spirit.

Here is a pic of Haunted Hall, the scaryest school in the world (opening soonly):

I am not drawing a pic of Uncle Bigbad, because 1) he is too crool, and 2) you cannot see ghosts, except after midnight.

I will draw me with Yeller, my best friend and cuz, instead:

a is just us being normal (Yeller is the loud 1). b is us dressed up as bossy Heads saying, "No chewing gum in class," etc.

Now I will do Stubbs the crowchick:

a is him being all proud of 2 new feathers.
b is him doing loop-the-loops in his glow-mask.

And now just 1 more:
a Small Horror of
Haunted Hall in his
spooksuit. Guess who?
Yes, Smellybreff, my baby
bro, going, "Sob, sob, I want
my mummy." (Only joking—
he likes it here, really.)

Yours cubly,
L. Wolf
(son and co-Head)

Dear Mom and Dad,

Your crool letter says my drawings are cubbish. I only did them to make Dad's fang feel better. Whyo Y is he so cross? Because I would not do a pic of his horrible dead bro, I bet.

So all right. Here he is haunting our cellar in the nighttime:

He only comes if he smells lovely bakebeans cooking in the pot. HMMM, YES PLEASE! CHOMP, CHOMP. He says they give him lots of Spirit Force.

12

Mom asks does he still look like Dad? Well, he looks just like before he died of the jumping beanbangs, only now you can see through him. He has a big, horrible furry face, plus big, horrible red eyes, plus big, horrible yellow teeth, and dribble dribbling down. Also, his eyebrows meet in the middle like Dad's, only they are more caterpillary. Plus he is all green, and ~~Doomy luminous~~ he glows in the dark. He is very fearsum, plus he makes your fur stand up.

He likes to come slidingly through the wall saying a terrible "WOOOOO!" and "GGGGRRRRAAAH!" Also he likes saying terrible words like this:

I AM THE GHOST OF UNCLE BIGBAD!
ME WHO DIED OF THE JUMPING BEANBANGS!
I DROOL, I DROOL FOR A LUVLY GOBFULL!
FETCH ME THE SHOVEL AND FEED ME SWIFTLY!

13

But if you say, "Uncle would you like to be our School Spirit and teach our pupils your ghosty powers?" he says:

NO! 2 MUCH LIKE BLINKING BLUNKING HARD WORK.

Then he gobbles his bakebeans (canteen size) and off he vanishes.

Yours unhelpedly,

L. Wolf (Head)

HAUNTED HALL
FOR SMALL HORRORS

Dear Mom and Dad,

Today Uncle said he might help us, but only if we vacuum his grave, plus change the writing on his gravestone—boo, shame, because it was good rhyming, and true. It said:

Bigbad Wolf
is dead at last
he died of eating
beans too fast

Now he made us do:

Dear Bigbad Wolf,
we miss him so
Do not be dead
oh drat oh blow.
M. I. P.

Yours wornoutly,

L.

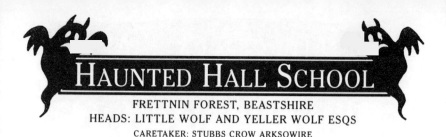

HAUNTED HALL SCHOOL

FRETTNIN FOREST, BEASTSHIRE
HEADS: LITTLE WOLF AND YELLER WOLF ESQS
CARETAKER: STUBBS CROW ARKSQWIRE

Dear Mom and Dad,

Nifty new notepaper, huh?

Uncle appeared again for some bakebeans.

He said, **"TELL ME (SLURP) WHAT STYLE OF SCHOOL YOU WISH TO OPEN. IF I LIKE THE SOUND OF IT (GULP), I MAY POSSIBLY APPEAR IN IT, YOU NEVER KNOW. IF I HAVE NOTHING MORE PROMISING ON MY CALENDAR (CHOMP)."**

So we told our ideas to him:

1) Yeller and me are the Co-Heads.
We do all the Bossing Around.

2) Stubbs is our teacher of how to make
spooksuits, and of flying lessons. Also he is
Caretaker and Fixy Boy with

his clever beak. Plus he
wants to be Bell Bird by
flying up to the bell tower
and going *ding* on the bell
(saves rope).

3) Smells is just a Small Horror
(like normal—har, har). His bear
can be too if he wants.

4) Our most important thing
is lots of thrilly fun and laughs
for all the teachers and pupils.

5) Lots of midnight feasts of
bakebeans (Uncle's best
snack).

Uncle said, **"CHOMP, SLURP, AND WHAT DO YOU EXPECT ME TO DO FOR YOU?"**

I said, "Uncle, Frettnin Forest is a fearsum place for small brute beasts. Thus and therefore, it is very handy to learn What to Do if a Big Scary Thing Tries to Get You. Their moms and dads want them to be ruff, tuff horrors, too. So will you be our School Spirit and teach us some tricks and ghosty powers? Like Popping Up Quick and Scary Laffing?

Uncle said, **"SNIFF SNUFF SNY,
WHAT DO I SPY? I SPY FLIPPING
FLOPPING HARD LABOR! YOU WISH ME
TO SHARE MY SPIRIT POWERS? AND
BE A TAME TERROR TO TRAIN YOUR
PUPILS? GRRRR, NO! I HATE SHARING,
ALSO, I AM SO MIGHTY, YOUR SMALL
PUPILS WOULD NEVER STAND UP TO
THE SHOCK OF ME!!"**

Yeller said quick, "UNCLE, WE REALLY WANT YOU SHOWIN' OFF YOUR POWERS, NOT SHARIN'. ALSO, CAN'T YOU TURN YOUR TERROR DOWN A LITTLE BIT?"

Uncle said, "HMMM (GULP), SHOWING OFF? YES, I DO LIKE THE SOUND OF THAT. I LOVE SHOWING OFF. WELL MAYBE I'LL CONSIDER IT. BUT YOU MUST DOUBLE MY RATION OF (BURP) LOVELY BAKEBEANS. THEY ARE SO GOOD FOR MY SPIRIT FORCE. AND YOU CAN TIDY THIS BLINKING BLUNKING PLACE UP. IT'S A DISGRRRRRACE!"

Not fair.

Yours discustardly,
Little

P.S. You ask what the M.I.P. is
for on Uncle's new gravestone?
Answer: Moan in Peace.

Dear Bigbad Wolf,
We miss him so
Do not be dead
oh drat oh blow.
M. I. P.

HAUNTED HALL SCHOOL

FRETTNIN FOREST, BEASTSHIRE
HEADS: LITTLE WOLF AND YELLER WOLF ESQS
CARETAKER: STUBBS CROW ARKSQWIRE

Dear Mom and Dad,

Phew! Work, work, work! Clean the blackboard, swat the flies, polish the desks, shoo the spiders, scrub the floors, windows, and bathrooms. Also, I have to sweep out the cellar so it is spiffy enuf for Uncle's grate self to appear in. He is a big lazy ghost and a greedyguts 2. The only things he does are lie in his grave and eat bakebeans.

Us worky boys are hungry and starving. We're not even allowed to eat any yummy bakebeans because they are only for Uncle's Spirit Force. We were saving them for rainy days and for being poor, like now, with no money from our pupils. Boo, shame.

So please send rabbit rolls and mice pies.

Yours rumblytumly,

Littly

Dear Mom and Dad,

The rabbit rolls and mice pies were yumshus. Yeller and me love them, kiss kiss. Smells saves all the tails and whiskers till last, then he eats them 2 quick and gets a coff – so cubbish! Also, Stubbs says, "Ark," meaning thanks for the cheese. It was ark-stra speshial.

But why o Y do you say I have let the pack down by being poor again? Anyway, who put rockets under my safe and blew it up into small smithers? Who made my gold go raining all over Frettnin Forest so nobody can find it now? Answer: your darling baby pet, Smellybreff. But you never blame him, do you?

But now listen to this, cuz it's good news. Yeller has made up a fine ad for us, saying:

ARRROOOO! Look out Richness, we are after you again!

Yours chestoutly,
L. Wolf, esqwire

Dear Mom and Dad,

Will you write and tell Smellybreff not to be a ~~moosink~~ ~~newsance~~ pain? Because me, Yeller, and Stubbs are trying and trying to please Uncle to get him to be our School Spirit and Terror, and Smells keeps messing all our things up. Also, we must rush around pantingly, putting up our posters all over Frettnin Forest.

Tell him he must just play with his ted like a normal small bro and not keep asking to be a Co-Head like me and Yeller. He thinks he is grown up, just because he got his

25

Silver Daring Deed Award for Clues and Courage when he was cubnapped by Mister Twister. But he is still 2 whiny and hopeless to play teachers with us. What do you think?

Your busywizzy boy,

L.

P.S. How about a nice surprise for us, hint hint? Like some Ratflakes or Moosepops, maybe?

HAUNTED HALL SCHOOL

FRETTNIN FOREST, BEASTSHIRE
HEADS: LITTLE WOLF AND YELLER WOLF ESQS
Deputy Head: Smellybreff Wolf Esq
CARETAKER: STUBBS CROW ARKSQWIRE

Dear Mom and Dad,

Thank you for your LOUD REPLY in red ink. Ooo-er. So yes, you're right. Smells must have his own way. Plus he can have a Deputy Head Badge if you want, plus be a Sir. Yes, I do remember he is your darling baby pet. And tell Dad yes, I do know what GOING RAVING MAD means, so he doesn't need to come on a long journey to show me. Thank you wunce morely.

Yours toldoffly,

L.

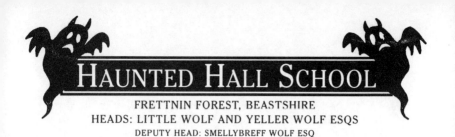

HAUNTED HALL SCHOOL

FRETTNIN FOREST, BEASTSHIRE
HEADS: LITTLE WOLF AND YELLER WOLF ESQS
DEPUTY HEAD: SMELLYBREFF WOLF ESQ
CARETAKER: STUBBS CROW ARKSQWIRE

Dear Mom and Dad,

I said Smells could be our Deputy Head like you made me. But can you just tell him no more spanking people, and stop saying, "Bend over, swish," all the time?

Yours stungly,
L. Wolf (Head)

HAUNTED HALL SCHOOL

FRETTNIN FOREST, BEASTSHIRE
HEADS: LITTLE WOLF AND YELLER WOLF ESQS
DEPUTY HEAD: SMELLYBREFF WOLF ESQ
CARETAKER: STUBBS CROW ARKSQWIRE

Dear Mom and Dad,

Your photo of Dad saying, "PACK IN THAT SPANKING, SON," arrived today. I showed it to Smells, and guess what? It made him howl headoffly. Then he jumped in the cupboard and *slam* went the door.

I said to Yeller and Stubbs, "That was a good scare for him. He will stop hitting us now, I bet."

Sad to say, he was just looking for some scissors. Now he has cut up your photo plus our curtains, tablecloth, etc.

Yours curtainlessly,
Little●-

Haunted Hall School

FRETTNIN FOREST, BEASTSHIRE
HEADS: LITTLE WOLF AND YELLER WOLF ESQS
DEPUTY HEAD: SMELLYBREFF WOLF ESQ
CARETAKER: STUBBS CROW ARKSQWIRE

Dear Mom and Dad,

Good thing Smells found those scissors! He says Cutting Things Up is his best thing now, plus Stubbs has trained him to do gluework. So now Smells says we must call him Mister Sticker and let him be a busy cub making stickers all day. He likes football the best, so lucky for us there are about 1 million "Wolf Sports Weekly" in the shed for him to cut up and glue.

Phew! Now Yeller and me can do some proper thinking up ideas for our new scary school without *swish, ouch!* every time we bend over.

Your cumfy
L. W.

30

HAUNTED HALL SCHOOL

FRETTNIN FOREST, BEASTSHIRE
HEADS: LITTLE WOLF AND YELLER WOLF ESQS
DEPUTY HEAD: SMELLYBREFF WOLF ESQ
CARETAKER: STUBBS CROW ARKSQWIRE

Dear Mom and Dad,

Oh drat and blow. We put up those ads for our school in Frettnin Forest 2 days ago, and still not 1 pupil has come. Y? I will tell you. It is because somebody has stuck Wanted posters all over our ads, that is Y! They are posters for Mister Twister the fox, saying:

WANTED
MISTER TWISTER
HE IS CUNNING,
HE IS NASTY
ALSO HE IS THE BEST
MASTER OF DISGUISE
IN BEASTSHIRE
—
BIG REWARD FOR CAPTURE

3 boos for a whopping, flopping fib! Because what about Uncle Bigbad? He is a lot more cunninger, crooler, and worster. And he is a brilliant dizgizzer if he tries his hardest. Plus he has lots of secret powers, I bet. It's only that he hates sharing, and that he is 2 busy at the moment being a lazy loafer.

Yours insultedly,

Little

HAUNTED HALL SCHOOL

FRETTNIN FOREST, BEASTSHIRE
HEADS: LITTLE WOLF AND YELLER WOLF ESQS
DEPUTY HEAD: SMELLYBREFF WOLF ESQ
CARETAKER: STUBBS CROW ARKSQWIRE

Dear Mom and Dad,

Felt sad all day because Mister Twister's
Wanted posters made our ads feel Unwanted.
But then Yeller had a brilliant idea! Make
Uncle jealous! Because then maybe he will
want to show off and be helping to us!

So at the *bong* of
midnight, when Uncle
came sniffsnuffingly after
his best snack (bakebeans,
canteen size), Yeller said
justwonderingly, "I WAS
JUST WONDERIN', UNCLE, DO YOU
THINK MISTER TWISTER MIGHT
GET A LOT FAYMUSSER THAN YOU,
WHAT WITH YOU LYIN' IN YOUR
GRAVE MOST OF THE TIME?"

33

Uncle said, "GRRRRR! THAT IS UTTER TWIDDLE AND TWODDLE. I AM THE GREAT STAR, FORMERLY KNOWN AS BIGBAD WOLF!! EVERYBODY KNOWS AND FEARS ME. I CAN DO FAR MORE CUNNING TRICKS THAN THAT MERE FOX! I CAN DO BUMPS IN THE NIGHT. I CAN DO WALKING THROUGH LUMPY OBJECTS. I CAN SMASH CHINA BY REMOTE CONTROL. I CAN DO GHASTLY HOWLS AND FEARSUM LAFFS, NOT TO MENTION GOING HEADLESS AND OTHER MIGHTY SPIRIT POWERS, LIKE FINDING LOST TREASURE."

Yeller said, "DID YOU SAY, 'FINDIN' LOST TREASURE'?"

Uncle said, **"GRRRRR AND BLAST! DID I SAY MY POWER OF FINDING LOST TREASURE? YOU MADE THAT SLIP OUT BY MAKING ME JEALOUS, YOU BLINKING BLUNKERS! WELL, YOU CAN FORGET ABOUT ME SHARING THAT POWER! JUST GET BUSY! FETCH ME CROWDS OF ADMIRERS, SWIFTLY, SWIFTLY, SO THAT I CAN THRILL AND AMAZE THEM WITH MY MIGHTYNESS!"**

Arrroooo! He is helpful to us at last! Have to hurry— new posters needed! Yours thinkythinkly, Little

HAUNTED HALL SCHOOL

FRETTNIN FOREST, BEASTSHIRE
HEADS: LITTLE WOLF AND YELLER WOLF ESQS
DEPUTY HEAD: SMELLYBREFF WOLF ESQ
CARETAKER: STUBBS CROW ARKSQWIRE

Dear Mom and Dad,

Yeller and me did loads of new posters. Phew! What a lot of drawing, writing, and coloring-in, etc! All that work, and no nice dinner after. Boo, shame (hint hint).

Stubbs did bring some chestnuts he collected from Frettnin Forest.

Yeller said all down and dumpy, "THANKS, STUBBS. BUT WOLF CUBS DO NOT EAT PRICKLY CHESTNUCKS."

Stubbs said, "Ark, Prrark," meaning, they are not for eating, they are for prarktiss! He wanted us to go to the classroom and sit the chestnuts down at the desks. He said we could pretend they were hedgehogs adding up sums, then boss them around. Chestnuts do not put up their hands and call you sir, but it's true they are very good for saying Headly things to, like, "Tuck your shirt in, sonny."

Smells got jealous and says he is not Mister Sticker anymore—he is Mister Woodcutter. Stubbs made him a playcabin in the dining room, and Yeller let him borrow the chopper. And so we don't have many chairs and tables left, I'm afraid. Maybe you want Smells back at the lair quite soonly?

Yours beggingly,
     Littly Wittly (snuggle snuggle)

P.S. This is a pic of what our pantry is like (bare—get it?) Please send more grub: rabbit rolls, shredded shrews, moosepops, plus something for Stubbs. And do you think you could find some cans of bakebeans (canteen size)? We are getting short of them. Boo, shame. Try looking for some in a cub scout camping place. But no eating them (the cub scouts, I mean). Har, har.

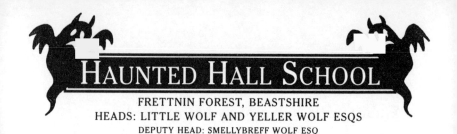

HAUNTED HALL SCHOOL

FRETTNIN FOREST, BEASTSHIRE
HEADS: LITTLE WOLF AND YELLER WOLF ESQS
DEPUTY HEAD: SMELLYBREFF WOLF ESQ
CARETAKER: STUBBS CROW ARKSQWIRE

Dear Mom and Dad,

Thanks for the grub. The deerdrops, moosepops and ratflakes were yummy, and so were the hamster loops and gerbil crunch. Yum, tasty! Stubbs says, "Ark," for the arkscellent maggot mix. No bakebeans? Too bad. (Don't tell Uncle we've got only a few left.)

We have put up our new posters in Frettnin Forest. Paws crossed there are no more Wanted Mister Twister posters to cover them up.

I am writing my quietest and most notdisturbly, because Yeller is making up something clever. A Kwestion Hare, I think it is called. It is not an ad, but it's a new way to tempt the moms and dads of Frettnin Forest to send small brute beasts to Haunted Hall. Also it is going to mention about our Entrance Test (our test to get in).

Arrroooo! Yeller's ideas are just the best! Because the moms and dads will say to their small brutes, "Oh goodie! A test for you, and you are such a brilliant cheater."

Yours mercy-boo-coo-ly,
moi (French)

HAUNTED HALL SCHOOL

FRETTNIN FOREST, BEASTSHIRE
HEADS: LITTLE WOLF AND YELLER WOLF ESQS
DEPUTY HEAD: SMELLYBREFF WOLF ESQ
CARETAKER: STUBBS CROW ARKSQWIRE

Dear Mom and Dad,

At sunjump today, Stubbs went highflying to drop Yeller's Kwestion Hares all over the forest. Paws crossed for lots of replies. By the way, Yeller says maybe some parents can pay in bakebeans instead of fees. Good, hm? Because that will help keep Uncle a happy haunter.

I'm sending 1 Kwestion Hare for you to see. It's a little bit smudjy (sorry), because Smells spit on it (jealous). Yeller's writing is also a bit hilly.

Yours rushly,

Little

40

KWESTION HARE
ABOUT HAUNTED HALL

* ? * ? * ? * ? * ? *

IMPORTANT KWESTIONS FOR PROUD
PARENTS FROM L AND Y WOLF, CO-HEADS,
HAUNTED HALL SCHOOL, FRETTNIN FOREST
(DO YOUR TOOTHMARK OR CHECK IN 1 BOX
ONLY)

CAN YOU READ? (TRICK QUESTION)
YES ☐   NO ☐   MY BRANE IS 2 SMALL ☐

HAVE YOU GOT MONEY FOR FEES
(NOT FOR FLEAS)
YES, LOADS ☐
NO, WE ARE A bit SAD & POOR ☐

IF NO MONEY, WILL YOU PAY IN
bAKEbEANS?
NO ☐   YES, BIG CANFULLS ☐

IS YOUR CUB, PUP, FLEDGIE, ETC. JUST A
WEAKY?
YES ☐   NO ☐

DO YOU WANT HIM LEARNIN TUFFNESS OR
JUST CURLIN UP OR HIDIN DOWN HOLES?
TUFF ☐   CURL UP ☐   HOLE HIDER ☐

DO YOU WANT HIM LEARNIN GOOD
HAUNTY POWERS AND SURVIVAL TRICKS
FROM A PROPER GHOST SUCH AS BIGBAD
WOLF, OR JUST NORMAL BORIN LESSONS?
HAUNTIN AND TRICKS ☐   BORIN STUFF ☐

DO YOU WANT HIM BEIN A HORROR OF
HAUNTED HALL, OR JUST GOING TO A
NO GOOD SCHOOL?
HAUNTED HALL, THE BEST, SCARYEST
SCHOOL IN THE WORLD ☐ ANY OLD DUMP ☐

WILL YOUR SMALL BRUTE COME FOR OUR
ENTRANCE TEST?
PROBLY ☐   DEFFNLY ☐   MAYBE ☐

IN A SHORT WAY, SAY WHAT HE/SHE/IT
NEEDS TEACHIN MOST (ANSWER IN BEST
PICS OR WRITIN, NO PAWPRINTS)

HAUNTED HALL SCHOOL

FRETTNIN FOREST, BEASTSHIRE
HEADS: LITTLE WOLF AND YELLER WOLF ESQS
DEPUTY HEAD: SMELLYBREFF WOLF ESQ
CARETAKER: STUBBS CROW ARKSQWIRE

Dear Mom and Dad,

ARRROOOO!!

Stubbs just flew in the window with a Kwestion Hare filled in by a dad weasel! He has checked the YES, LOADS OF MONEY box (arrroooo x 3!) Also, he likes the look of Haunted Hall. Look at his answer to SAY WHAT HE/SHE/IT NEEDS TEACHIN' MOST:

Our pup Throttler is a blot on the family. He has gone Veggie. We will pay big munny if you be strict teachers and teach him to be a propper bludthirsty weasly boy again.

Plus he checked the DEFFNLY box for doing the Entrance Test! Just wait till Uncle hears. He will go *thrill thrill* I bet!

Yours zestfully,
Littly

HAUNTED HALL SCHOOL

FRETTNIN FOREST, BEASTSHIRE
HEADS: LITTLE WOLF AND YELLER WOLF ESQS
DEPUTY HEAD: SMELLYBREFF WOLF ESQ
CARETAKER: STUBBS CROW ARKSQWIRE

Dear Mom and Dad,

I am all upset. I did not know wolfs are s'posed to look down on weasels. But Uncle says they are common riffraff and much 2 easy to impress.

He says, **"YOU SEEM TO BE FORGETTING THAT I AM THE STAR ATTRACTION AND TERROR AROUND HERE! I DEMAND A BETTER CLASS OF CREATURE TO PRAISE MY SPLENDIDNESS."**

Oh, boo. Now Uncle says no more public appearances from him. Also no helping with Entrance Tests unless 1) we promise xtra helpings of bakebeans from now on, and 2) we gloom the place up a bit.

He says 2) is to remind him of his lovely grave, but really he is only showing his spite. Just because we just finished getting HH all neat and cheery, I bet!

Yours sinkingly,
    Little

HAUNTED HALL SCHOOL

FRETTNIN FOREST, BEASTSHIRE
HEADS: LITTLE WOLF AND YELLER WOLF ESQS
DEPUTY HEAD: SMELLYBREFF WOLF ESQ
CARETAKER: STUBBS CROW ARKSQWIRE

Dear Mom and Dad,

Phew! Just time for a short note because of working and working to make the place more gloomish. No more electric things for us— Uncle says candles are heaps better for shivery shadows.

1 good thing has happened from this. Smells has stopped being Mister Woodcutter (lucky, because yesterday he unmade 6 beds in the dorm going *chipchop* with his chopper).

Now candles are his best thing. He wants us to call him Mister Waxworks, because he chews candles up soft and makes models from them. So far he has made just blobs, but he calls them faymus TV stars, footballers, etc. Such a cub.

Yours grownupply,

L. Wolf

HAUNTED HALL SCHOOL

FRETTNIN FOREST, BEASTSHIRE
HEADS: LITTLE WOLF AND YELLER WOLF ESQS
DEPUTY HEAD: SMELLYBREFF WOLF ESQ
CARETAKER: STUBBS CROW ARKSQWIRE

Dear Mom and Dad,

So nice today! You would not beleeeve how many answers to Kwestion Hares Stubbs has flown in. Lots of them say YES to paying large fees just for the chance to learn tuffness tricks and ghosty powers from us and Uncle!

Yeller is just back from a spider hunt. He found buckets of fat, tickly 1s—perfect for making nice, sticky webs and hiding lurkingly down drainholes, inkwells, etc.

Stubbs helped me do a fine banner for waving from our flagpole on the bell tower, saying:

HAUNTED HALL ENTRANCE TEST
This Sat. at Ghosty time
Be there and have a good scare

We have done a fine job putting *eee-aaahs* in the doors. Next we must do some *creeeeks* in the floor, plus make all the radiators go *blugblug ticktap* in the night. Uncle will be all swelled up with proudness, I bet. So he will probly say:

GRRRR! I AM SO PLEASED, I WILL SHOW YOU MY POWER OF FINDING LOST TREASURE!

Smells is doing car alarm noises. He thinks it helps.

Yours deffly,
Little

HAUNTED HALL SCHOOL

FRETTNIN FOREST, BEASTSHIRE
HEADS: LITTLE WOLF AND YELLER WOLF ESQS
DEPUTY HEAD: SMELLYBREFF WOLF ESQ
CARETAKER: STUBBS CROW ARKSQWIRE

Dear Mom and Dad,

Everything is almost ready for Entrance Test Day. Only 2 nights to go.

Yeller has given the cellar a more dungeonish smell with cabbage water and by poking old cheese into cracks.

I went on a spooky chain hunt, but not much luck. Just got the 1s off our bikes—not clanky enuff. BUT (big but) I have made all our family portraits of Uncles, Grandads etc. a lot better. By putting swivelly eyes in them, they follow you round the room.

50

Good, huh? My next job is to make some secret panels so we can play Hide and Skweak. Get it?

Stubbs's clever beak has got Smells busy! Because, guess what? He made 2 Action-cub battlesuits—1 is for him, and 1 is for his ted. He also put up the tent in the back garden. Arrroooo! Now Smells can live outside and not be in our way! He can chew his candles, make his waxworks, and do car alarm noises all he likes.

Yours muchbetterly,

Little

NeeeeNaaaa?

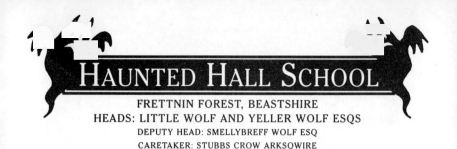

HAUNTED HALL SCHOOL

FRETTNIN FOREST, BEASTSHIRE
HEADS: LITTLE WOLF AND YELLER WOLF ESQS
DEPUTY HEAD: SMELLYBREFF WOLF ESQ
CARETAKER: STUBBS CROW ARKSQWIRE

Dear Mom and Dad,

Tomorrow night is the night. Crowds of brutes are coming, so Uncle can have a good show off and we can have lots of fun. Stubbs is here saying, "Ark," meaning, send a few arksamples. So I am.

Arksample 1, a small tortoise is coming. His mom thinks he is 2 shy, so he needs a good shocking to get him more out of his shell.

Arksample 2, Mister Webfoot is sending a jamjarfull of his frogspawn jellydots from the pond up by Lake Lemming. He thinks a scary school will help turn them into tadpoles.

52

Nextly, 3 fraidy bats. Their dad is fed up with buying nightlights and asks, Can we get them used to the dark?

Mrs. Rattlesnake wants a lot of strictness for her young Squirmer. He has a bad habit of sucking his rattle and it gets 2 soggy.

Loads more have filled in our KHs, and Smells has captured 6 bugs and insects that came creepingly to his tent. (He made a mini waxworks Chamber of Horrors on a tray to attract them. Then he went, "Har, har, gotcha," and popped them into his matchbox.)

Yours hummingly,

Mmm mm (guess who?)

HAUNTED HALL SCHOOL

FRETTNIN FOREST, BEASTSHIRE
HEADS: LITTLE WOLF AND YELLER WOLF ESQS
DEPUTY HEAD: SMELLYBREFF WOLF ESQ
CARETAKER: STUBBS CROW ARKSQWIRE

Dear Mom and Dad,

Here is 1 of our Entrance Test papers for you to see:

ENTRANCE TEST PAPER
FOR HAUNTED HALL SCHOOL

TASK 1:
Sit quietly in the dark and wait for a ghost to pop out. No lickwashes, no scratching, no chewing test papers.

TASK 2:
When ghost comes, do your loudest WOO!

TASK 3:

See how quick you can dig a hole with an Entrance to it. Pop down it. Say, "Well done, me. I have passed my Entrance. That was an easy test! Now I can be a pupil and give heaps of my dad's riches to Haunted Hall!"

TASK 4:

Pop back, then draw a nice pic of our Haunted Hall ghost.

TASK 5:

Learn the Haunted Hall School Song and sing fortissimo (your head off). This is it:

we are the Horrors of Haunted Hall
Spooky are we, we are not scared at all
No matter how tuff other brute beasts are
we are more crafty, so nah nah nah!

Do you like it? Now we are all ready and
Uncle is 2. We have told him, "Do not
forget to appear just on the bong of
midnight tomorrow night, like normal. Only
do not be 2 scary, because remember that 2
much jitters might make small brutes run
away from Haunted Hall."

I am sure he will not appear 2 harshly.
Because he promised, saying:

WHO ME? WOULD I?

Yours trustingly,

L.

HAUNTED HALL SCHOOL

FRETTNIN FOREST, BEASTSHIRE
HEADS: LITTLE WOLF AND YELLER WOLF ESQS
DEPUTY HEAD: SMELLYBREFF WOLF ESQ
CARETAKER: STUBBS CROW ARKSQWIRE

Dear Mom and Dad,

I am all upset. Our Entrance Test was so good, then Smells and Uncle let us down.

We had such a big long line outside the front gate! And that was only just after the sun hid. By midnight, phew!—what a whopping big crowd!

So Yeller and me put on our Headly looks, saying (stern voices), "All hold hands in 2s. Then quickmarch to the cellar and sit up straight in nice rows." Stubbs was everso good at caretaking. He pulled the blinds down, mopped up sick-ups, and took wrigglers to the lavs.

We let Smells stir the bakebeans in the pot and give out some Test papers. Then guess what he went and did? He opened his matchbox up and said to his captured bugs and insects, "Hello, I am Mister Sticker," then he glued them to the fridge.

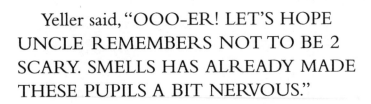

That made all the other pupils go jumping around saying, "Help it's a trap! Help! Save me from being a fridge sticker!" etc.

Yeller said, "OOO-ER! LET'S HOPE UNCLE REMEMBERS NOT TO BE 2 SCARY. SMELLS HAS ALREADY MADE THESE PUPILS A BIT NERVOUS."

Up went the lovely steam of bakebeans (tempt, tempt) from the pot. Then, *BONG!* It was midnight, and all of a suddenly, right on time, Uncle appeared.

But he did not even try not to be 2 scary!
He did not come in like a normal ghost
at all. He came in going:

**CRACKLE
FIZZ
FUME
FLASH!!**

Because he was dressed
up as a big raging
forest fire!!!

Your feeless boy,
L. Wolf

Haunted Hall School

FRETTNIN FOREST, BEASTSHIRE
HEADS: LITTLE WOLF AND YELLER WOLF ESQS
DEPUTY HEAD: SMELLYBREFF WOLF ESQ
CARETAKER: STUBBS CROW ARKSQWIRE

Dear Mom and Dad,

Did I tell about all our small pupils running away
very very very very swiftly? Then Uncle said,

**"GRRRAAAH HAR HAR! WASN'T I
FANTASTIC, THE WAY I MADE ALL
THOSE PINK LITTLE
BEASTS GO CHARGING
BACK TO THEIR HOLES?"**

Yeller replied, "THEY WEREN'T PINK
WHEN THEY CAME IN. THAT WAS
ONLY BECAUSE YOU SHOCKED
THEM OUT OF THEIR SKINS! LOOK
AT ALL THESE TINY FURRY SUITS
LYIN' ABOUT ON THE FLOOR. NOW
WE SHALL HAVE TO MAIL
THEM ALL BACK TO

THEIR MOMS AND DADS. AND NOT
ALL OF THEM HAVE GOT THEIR
NAMES SEWN IN THEM."

Uncle just laffed his hollow laff, saying,

**"HOOO, HAR HAR! I HAVEN'T HAD
SUCH A GOOD TIME SINCE I DEVOURED
THE MAILMAN! BUT NOW TELL ME
HONESTLY, WASN'T I JUST TERRIFYING
AS A FOREST FIRE? DIDN'T YOU JUST
LOVE THE WAY I FRIGHTENED
THAT SKINNY GRAY YOUNG
FELLOW? I MADE HIM
GO SCUTTLING
UP THE CHIMNEY!"**

I said, "Uncle, he was just a small, shy
tortoise. You were s'posed to bring him out
of his shell gently. But no, you made him slip
out like wet soap. It will take us ages fitting
him back in. And what about the Red

Admiral butterfly you shocked into a Cabbage White?"

Uncle said, **"ANOTHER MASTERSTROKE! YES, I BELIEVE THAT HAPPENED WHEN I TRANSFORMED MYSELF INTO A PACK OF HOUNDS. CONGRATULATE ME, SWIFTLY, SWIFTLY, ON THAT SPLENDIDLY DARK POWER! THAT WAS THE FIRST TIME I HAVE TRIED DIVIDING MYSELF AND HOWLING FROM MANY PLACES. MOST EFFECTIVE, WASN'T I? THANK YOU, THANK YOU!"**

I said, "But Uncle, you promised to appear gently. Those dark powers you did were 2 harsh."

Uncle said, **"STOP WHINING, VILE FLUFFBALL! YOU ARE GETTING ON MY**

NERVES, SPOILING MY HORRID FUN! AND I WANT MORE! THOSE LITTLE SQUEAKERS WERE FAR TOO EASY TO SCARE! THEY ARE A WASTE OF GOOD TERROR, SO NOW YOU MUST MAKE A BET WITH ME."

I said, "What sort of a bet, Uncle?"

He said, "I BET YOU MY POWER OF FINDING LOST TREASURE THAT YOU CAN'T FETCH ME ANY BRUTE BIG ENOUGH OR BRAVE ENOUGH TO STAND UP TO ME DOING MY DARKEST AND DIRTIEST, SHALL WE SAY FOR 5 MINUTES?"

Yeller said, "BUT THAT IS A HARD BET FOR US. WHAT IF WE LOSE?"

Uncle said, "TUFF! IF YOU LOSE, I SHALL BECOME ALL SULKY AND NOT HELP YOU

AT ALL, AND THAT WILL SERVE YOU RIGHT FOR MAKING ME WORK SO HARD. I SHALL RETURN TO MY GRAVE FOREVER AND HAVE A WELL-DESERVED M.I.P.!"

I said, "But how can we have a Haunted Hall School without you?"

Uncle said, "EXACTLY! NOW BE SILENT, SPECK! I WILL GIVE YOU 3 TURNS OF THE MOON TO SEARCH, NO MORE. GRRRAH, HAR HAR!"

Oh dear. Uncle is such a teaser.

Yours headscratchingly,

L.

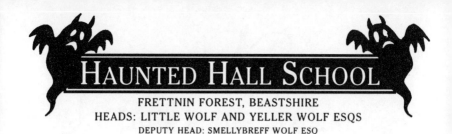

HAUNTED HALL SCHOOL

FRETTNIN FOREST, BEASTSHIRE
HEADS: LITTLE WOLF AND YELLER WOLF ESQS
DEPUTY HEAD: SMELLYBREFF WOLF ESQ
CARETAKER: STUBBS CROW ARKSQWIRE

The pantry

Dear Mom and Dad,

Help! We have looked and looked in every hole and hollow tree in Frettnin Forest and not 1 brute is brave enuff to stand up to Uncle's powers. So now I must travel MILES afar to find such a ruff, tuff creature.

Yeller wants to come with me but I said no, Smells needs looking after. Also, he must guard the school in case of robbers.

Uncle is horrid and lazy. Last night he could not even be bothered going back to his grave. He has moved into an old bottle he found in the pantry, just because it says "Powerful Spirit" on the label. He said:

So vain.

I must go to our library and look up Tuff Creatures.

Yours studyingly,

L.

HAUNTED HALL SCHOOL

FRETTNIN FOREST, BEASTSHIRE
HEADS: LITTLE WOLF AND YELLER WOLF ESQS
DEPUTY HEAD: SMELLYBREFF WOLF ESQ
CARETAKER: STUBBS CROW ARKSQWIRE

The library

Dear Mom and Dad,

Encyclopeedias are fat, did you know that? They are so heavy you have to use both paws for holding them, then get Stubbs to sit on your head and turn the pages for you with his clever beak. Too bad he is left-beaked, because it made him start from "Z" and work backwards, so it took ages to get to "A." And, oh no! "A" was just the letter we wanted for a ruff, tuff reptile!

Stubbs went, "Ark! Alark!!" meaning "A" is for Alarkgator!

Ooo-er! So now I must find 1 and bring it back to win the bet against Uncle, save Haunted Hall School, and discover the power to find my lost gold. But sad to say the nearest alarkgator lives many miles away in Yellowsmoke Swamplands. That is in Grimshire! How can I get there and back with an alarkgator in just 3 turns of the moon? Yellowsmoke Swamplands takes 7 turns of the moon to run there and back, maybe 8!

Yours stumpedly,
L.

HAUNTED HALL SCHOOL

FRETTNIN FOREST, BEASTSHIRE
HEADS: LITTLE WOLF AND YELLER WOLF ESQS
DEPUTY HEAD: SMELLYBREFF WOLF ESQ
CARETAKER: STUBBS CROW ARKSQWIRE

The dorm

Dear Mom and Dad,

Cannot sleep. Yeller has got paper all over the floor. He is scratching and scratching planningly with his pen. But it's 2 late, I fear. Stubbs is also a busy wideawaker. He is doing knitting plus making something from 1 of Yeller's inky plans. I do not know what, but there is canvas in it, tent poles, string, plus Yeller's kite with the wolf eyes on it.

I think maybe they are both just taking their minds off us being poor and starving forever. Because not even Yeller can think up a brilliant way to get to Yellowsmoke Swamplands AND come back with an alarkgator by Wensdie (cannot spell it).

Yours failedly,
Little

69

HAUNTED HALL SCHOOL

FRETTNIN FOREST, BEASTSHIRE
HEADS: LITTLE WOLF AND YELLER WOLF ESQS
DEPUTY HEAD: SMELLYBREFF WOLF ESQ
CARETAKER: STUBBS CROW ARKSQWIRE

Under tree in front garden

Dear Mom and Dad,

Something gulpish. Are you ready? Gulp. Stubbs says he wants to fly me to seek for an alarkgator!

He says, "Ark!" meaning, Arkshun Stations! Also he says he has grown two new tail feathers, so his flying is strong.

I said, "But Stubbs, you are only a crowchick, not even a full fledgie. Are you sure you can carry a passenger? Besides, how will we get a big, ruff, tuff reptile back here in just 3 turns of the moon?"

He just says, "Ark!" meaning, do not worry, he is an arkspert at flying now. He has also made a thing from Yeller's plan that is a secret invention to help us. But no time to arksplain now.

Yeller is upset not to come, but he must stay and do guarding in case of robbers, and be the minder of Smells.

Our crunchy snacks are packed, and I just put on my string harness that Stubbs knitted. We are ready. I just want to leave a small message for my grave in case of an emerjuncy:

Here lies L. Wolf
He fell off the sky
He was a bit 2 heavy
but never mind,
good try.

Your trembly boy,

Little

The sky, above Frettnin Forest, Beastshire

Dear Mom and Dad,

Sorry about the scribbuls, but this is a
flying air letter. We are up! Aayee, I love
highuppness! It is so thrilly, kiss kiss! The
wind takes your breff and pins your ears and
fur back. Stubbs is a strong airswimmer, but
he's getting a bit tired now. Frettnin Forest is
like moss below.

Now we are over the Parching Plain. It is
bumpy. Stubbs says, "Ark!" meaning, arkstra
hot air because of the burning sands. So
bouncy.

Poor Stubbs. I think he has got a

wing

Dear Mom and Dad,

We did a crashland, a dusty 1, but our bones stayed together. Lucky us, huh? It's so hot here. Phew! I am trying to make a shadow so Stubbs can cool off and get his strongness back. I wanted to read about Yeller's invention. There is a paper with it called 'Instruckshuns', but my head is busy having a think. Are there tuff and fearless brutes that live in Parching Plains? Maybe, and then we don't need to fly further, hm?

My thinks are up in the sky now. I can hear buzzards saying *keeee-keeee* in case we are a nice snack for them. Ooo-er! I remember now—buzzards are very fierce, with hooks for claws and sharp beaks. *Ding!* An idea has just jumped in my head! I will play dead and try to capture 1 when it comes down to eat me.

Yours backsoonly (I hope),
Little Snack (just kidding)

Dear Mom and Dad,

I really didn't like that buzzard coming up close. I made my eyes slits, but I saw him looking at my tasty parts. So I said, "'Scuse me, but I am just a small beakful, and so is my friend here. P'raps you would like to come back with us and meet my Uncle. He is a lot bigger."

The buzzard said, "*Kee-keee!* How big is hee-ee?"

I said, "Very big. Maybe you have heard of him. His name is BB Wolf."

And do you know what?
Off he went—*VOOOM*. Such a big softy. Lucky the wind from him voooming made Stubbs nice and cool. He is feeling a lot better!

Yours Readyfortakeoffly,
Little

The sky, cloudy part over some mountains

Dear Mom and Dad,

Brrrr! Broken Tooth Caves and Grim Mountains far under us. Can see roofs small as sparrows' nests—Hamneezia, maybe. We are so frozz up here now. Stubbs is flapping very hard. I must stop writing and make myself streamliney.

Yours cheekssuckedinly,
Little

Dear Mom and Dad,

Ooo-er! I fell asleep for a bit. When I woke up, I thought, "Oh no, I have turned into a polar bear cub sitting on a big seagull!" But do not fret and frown. It was just Stubbs and me flying through a blizzard.

1 good thing is that it will be a soft crash if we do fall, because the White Wildness is all snow. But paws crossed Stubbs can keep going as the crow flies, huh?

Yours fridgely,
Brittle (joke)

Dear Mom and Dad,

Phew! Landed
at Yellowsmoke
Swamplands,
but not
crashingly
because of the
swamp. Now a
bit mucky, but
Stubbs is my hero.

We are trying out Yeller's new invention
—a Tentyglider. It's brilliant! The
Instruckshuns are pretty hard, but if you fold
it 1 way you can do camping in it (the door
is Yeller's kite with the yellow wolf eyes on
it). And if you fold it a new way, it turns
into a glider. So Stubbs can tow even
whopping big brutes in it!

Camping out is my worst thing, even
with Stubbs for company. Bad things happen
in the night, like you hear the bogeywolf

coming up the stairs to get you. He goes
step, step, step, step, step. Then you wake up and
you think, phew—no stairs in here. It was
just a squirrel plopping nuts onto the roof.

More later from,

Yours widerawakely,
Little

Yellowsmoke Swamplands, up the grassy end

Dear Mom and Dad,

Later. No alarkgators yet, but we did find
a lion. He was hiding in the long grass.
Stubbs was upset because he had feathers on
his tongue, so we did not go 2 near.

I shouted out a 'scuse me to him, saying,
"Hmm, I don't s'pose you ever get scared, do
you?"

He said, "*SSPITTT RRRUMBLE
GGRRRAAAH! RRRR*idiculous idea!"

But when I asked about coming with us to our cellar to stand up to Uncle Bigbad's shocking powers for 5 minutes he said, "Er, d'you mean Bigbad Wolf? Dribbly feller, very bad temper? Um, well you see, I must have my wide open spaces. Otherwise I would come with you and do my bit for the pride, I honestly would. But cellars? No, no. Much too closed in, you follow me? And no nice long grasses to tickle my tummy. Good-bye." Then he ran away.

It's getting darkly dim now, but Mum always says: Yellow eyes are friends with the dark. So handy about our yellow wolf-eye door which is nice and scary. Also lucky our camp is on an island (we are safe from sharp teeth). Wish we had some islands in Frettnin Forest.

Yours yawnly (plus an "Ark" from Stubbs),

Little

Yellowsmoke Swamplands, on an island in a lake

Dear Mom and Dad,

You want to be careful about islands. Because sometimes they are alarkgators. And when you get up in the morning, better not go, "Hmm, breakfast, yum," just in case your island starts thinking breakfast thoughts 2.

Another thing: If you see a sort of green bridge going up in front of your eyes, do not walk across it, because it might be the alarkgator opening his mouth. Better if you stay where you are on his back and say, "Good thing I put this tent up on you because it makes you look so hansum." (Rule 3 of Badness: Fib your head off.)

I did hear a funny *vrroomba vrroomba* in my ear in the night, but I was 2 tired and cozy to get wurrid. Then this morning I found out the alarkgator just ate a small cub who was listening to his Walkwolf. That is Y his words have got a beat, like, "Jump in my pool, it's really cool."

I said to him, "Hello, I am L. Wolf Esqwire and this is S. Crow Arksqwire. We are here to tell you about a nice prize you have won in a raffle. It is a trip on a glider to visit a funny school. Would you like to come?" (More Rule 3.)

The alarkgator said:
"You don't fool me with your talk about a raffle, ha!
Get in my jaws and let me snaffle ya!"

I said, "You are very ruff-tuff. Are you scared of anybody? Like a wolf, maybe?"

The alarkgator said:
"My name is Snap, I am where it's at,
I'm a cool, cool alligator.
I am the jaw you can't ignore,
Catch you now, or catch you later!

Hope you don't mind if I say to you,
You'd be mighty good to chew.
You look tasty, you look crunchy,
How would you like to be my lunchy?"

I said, "Oh, all right." Because I
remembered another 1 of Mum's best
sayings, the 1 about how to get untangled if
you are in a prickly bush. She always says:
You must give to the blackberry bush before
he'll let you go. So I held Stubbs by the
wing and we jumped in the
alarkgator's mouth. And
guess what I gave him?
Answer: the
tent pole!

Arrroooo! He lashed and splashed and
splashed and lashed, but he *could* not eat me
and Stubbs for his lunchy—har, har.

Yours unchewedly,
Little

Near Broken Tooth Caves, Beastshire again

Dear Mom and Dad,

Do you know what? That alarkgator was just a big baby! He cried and cried just because me and Stubbs tricked him with the tent pole and he could not eat us. So there's no use gliding him back to HH to stand up to Uncle, because he would probly say "Boohoo, blub" right away, then Uncle would win his bet—boo, shame.

Now Stubbs and me are all gloomy and glum, because 2 turns of the moon have gone past already! We had a chat and we said Grimshire is no good, so we'd better go back to Beastshire. Stubbs said, "Ark!" meaning it's arkay with him.

He had to fly us back across The White Wildness, then over Mount Tester to Broken Tooth Caves. It was hard for him, but on and on he flew flappingly with no moaning, and we hit the land gentle as a leaf.

Sometimes you get outlaws here but I 'spect we will not see any. We have made the Tentyglider into a glider just in case. Now off we go into the caves with our flashlights burning.

Yours searchingly,
L.

Dark Hills (Windy Ridge side)

Dear Mom and Dad,

No luck finding outlaws, but guess what? A Mountain Ranger has come to help us. He has got sharp eyes, a pointy face, and a smell like pepper. His uniform is nice but it sticks out at the back.

He spoke softly to us saying, "You look like smart young laddies, and I have some questions for you. Will you gaze into my eyes and answer them?"

We did not know how to say no to him, so we told all about searching for a large brute that is not afraid of a certain faymus terror. He said, "My boys, you interest me strangely. Am I to understand that you are referring to that terrible crook and miser, Bigbad Wolf? He, they say, who died of the jumping beanbangs?"

I said a proud, "Yes," and Stubbs said, "Ark," meaning I arkgree with Little.

The Ranger said, "Amazing! What is his racket now?"

I said, "He does not play tennis. He is a shocking ghost and master of spirit dizgizzes, plus Star Attraction at Haunted Hall, the scaryest school in the world."

The Ranger said, "And where exactly is his residence?"

I said, "He has a very nice grave, but just lately he has moved into a bottle in the pantry at Haunted Hall. But when we can find a beast that is not scared of him for 5 minutes, he will tell us by Spirit Power where all my gold is hiding. So I will be rich wunce morely."

Then the Ranger got very peppery, and
he said that was very interesting. Now,
arrroooo, he says he knows a way to help us!
Because he knows a brute beast that is not
scared of anything. All we have got to do is
go with him to the edge of a very steep cliff
and wink down his telescope.

Goody! (I hate steepness, but I like
telescopes.) More later.

Your nosy boy,
Little

Steep cliff, Dark Hills, Beastshire

Dear Mom and Dad,

sorry about the nervous writing, but there is a bear, a big one

(behind us?).

It's goodby foreverly,
   L. Wolf

Bears' camp near a fast river, Dark Hills, Beastshire

Dear Mom and Dad,

Oh no! We are captured by bears, and it's all that Ranger's fault!

We were on a path just a small way down from the top of a

s

t

e

e

p cliff.

The Ranger said for us to look peepingly through the telescope at a boy and girl cub. They were standing in a roary river, fishing for salmon. You would not beleeeeve how strong they are for cubs, and they gave each other such fierce bites! The mom bear was there, but she was 2 busy chomping down honeycakes to watch them.

That Ranger was silly. He would not be still! He kept standing up so the sun flashed on his shiny buttons, and he kept coffing loud.

I said, "You want to be careful, because this path is thin. Just s'pose a huge big brute comes up behind us, and there is only room for 1 of us to escape quick!"

That was when Stubbs went, "Ark! Ick!" meaning, arkscape quick! Because the dad bear (whopping huge) was right behind us holding my tail tight. And guess who escaped quick? (Clue: not me or Stubbs.) Answer: the Ranger!

But just then came a loud scream. Stubbs shouted, "Ark!" meaning arkcident. The boy cub got swept away by the roary river!

Quick as a chick I said to the bear, "Let go of my tail and we will save your cub." So he did.

Now I know, Dad, you will say, "Whyo Y are you still captured? Y not flee away quick and say 'Har, har, I was fibbing my head off'?" Answer: we need that cub!

Yours daringdeedly,
Little

Dear Mom and Dad,

The boy cub nearly got lost in the rapids.
But Stubbs dropped me on him in the water
with Yeller's strong kite string tied to my
harness. I bit the fur on the bear cub's neck
and held on. Then Stubbs gave the other
end of the string to the dad bear. Even the
lazy mom bear stopped munching and came
to pull.

The dad and mom bear pulled and
pulled, then PLOP! out of the roary water
we came.

Then the dad bear whacked the boy bear
2 times, saying, "THAT's for being
knuckleheaded, and THAT's for next time."
Then the mom bear whacked him a hard 1
too. Then the girl cub bit him, then he bit
her back. And do you know what he said?
He said, "Rocks and rapids can't scare me! I
like banging my head on rocks! I did that on
purpose, so there!" And he gave me a hard
push out of the way and climbed up a tall,
tall tree.

His mom said, "Get down out of that tree, Normus! There are bees in that nest. They'll sting you all over!"

The boy cub said, "Bees don't scare me. I like getting stinged." Then he got stings in his nose plus on his tongue, and he just said, "Har, har. Doesn't hurt!"

It did hurt really, I bet— he was just showing off. Then he threw the hive at me to make the bees chase me.

This is Y I said we need that bear. He is a big bully, but I think he can win the bet against Uncle! I just hope his mom and dad will let him go with Stubbs and me.

Yours hopingly,
Little

Dear Mom and Dad,

I think the Bears have got more nasty tempers than Dad. (Only kidding, Dad—yours is the baddest.) So it was quite easy to take Normus away from them, because he gets on their nerves a lot. Also they say they do not know what to do with him. Maybe that is Y they did not eat me, plus they liked listening about me being a wolf cub and a proud Co-Head of Haunted Hall School.

Mr. Bear said to me, "So you're a wolf cub and he's a crowchick, eh? Funny, because I thought maybe you was just something the cat coffed up! And you're starting up a school, you say? Now I don't see that. I don't see you being a teacher at all. What I see is you covered in honey and spread on my sandwich. Unless you can prove you're not telling me big fat fibs!"

Quick as a chick I said, "Pay attention! Claws on lips, and come along!" like we did for practiss on the chestnuts.

Mrs. Bear said, "Ooh, he knows all the sayings, just like a proper teacher! Do some more!"

I said, "Now then! Sit up straight, and no chewing gum."

She said, "Ooh, he is good. Go on, Dad bear, let's send Normus away to his school. After all, he never learns from us, does he?"

Dad bear said, "How do we know it's a proper strict school with the right sort of School Spirit and all that?"

I said, "Haunted Hall has got the strictest most shockingest School Spirit in Beastshire. His name is BB Wolf."

Dad bear said, "Well that's all right then. And do you believe in short, sharp shocks?"

I said, "Oh yes."

Dad bear said, "Good. Just what he needs. The only way to get sense into him is to knock it in. So don't take any cheek from him. Show him the back of your paw. And a good sharp bite never does any harm. Does it, Normus?"

But Normus wasn't listening. He was wrestling with his sister for a can of peaches (canteen size). He grabbed it from her and opened it. Sideways. With his claws. Ooo-er.

Stubbs has finished putting the glider together. Hope Normus doesn't break it with his strongness.

Yours pawscrossedly,

L.

Shore of Lake Lemming, night of the 3rd moon

Dear Mom and Dad,

Such hard flying for Stubbs! He had me
in the harness and was towing the glider
behind. Phew! What a shouter that Normus
is—nearly loud as Yeller. He kept shouting,
"Higher higher! Gliding can't scare me!"

It was dark 2, and some cold rain spit at us.

Over Windy Ridge Stubbs flapped. The
air was so bumpy and frozz, it was like a
fight all the way to Lake Lemming. We were
wurrid when we got there, because there's
no runway to land on, and because of all the
dark trees on the edge of Frettnin Forest.

But good old Yeller—he was thinking of
us in the night. He did not want us going

"bash" into a tree. So he said to Smells,
"QUICK, MISTER
WAXWORKS!
RUN TO THE
SHORE OF THE
LAKE WITH YOUR
CANDLES AND YOUR
SHOVEL! WE MUST MAKE
2 TONS OF MOLEHILLS
AND PUT LIGHTS ON THEM."

That made a nice landing place, and
down went Stubbs and the glider behind
with Normus on it, all smooth and crashless.

Stubbs and me did 3 arrrooooos for joy
and said, "Well done and thanks, Yeller and
Smells!" But not Normus. He just gave
Yeller a frown and said, "Flying
can't scare me! I like crashing!"
Then he said to Smells,
"Hello, Stickybud.
Let's play Head
in Mouth—
you go 1st!"

Smells did not stay. He gave Normus 1 of his nasty looks. Then he took the shovel and ran off to his tent in the back garden.

I said to Normus, "No time for ruff, tuff games. We must hurry to school before midnight OR ELSE."

He just said, "OR ELSE what? You can't make me. Teachers can't scare me."

I said, "Good thing. I hope you are not scared of Uncle Bigbad either!"

Yours wishmeluckly,
Little

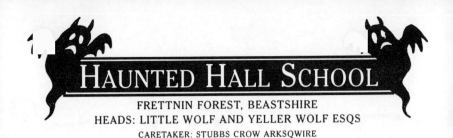

HAUNTED HALL SCHOOL

FRETTNIN FOREST, BEASTSHIRE
HEADS: LITTLE WOLF AND YELLER WOLF ESQS
CARETAKER: STUBBS CROW ARKSQWIRE

Dear Mom and Dad,

Back we went rushingly to Haunted Hall. We needed to heat up some bakebeans quick.

Haunted Hall was all glum and gloomy, but Normus did not seem to be 1 bit nervous. He just kept barging around saying, "Let's have a wrestle," etc., and getting in our way a lot.

Then Stubbs said, "Ark!" meaning hark, the bong of midnight! But Normus was not still. He pulled a big bunch of nice new feathers out of Stubbs's tail. Such a big bully!

Then all of a suddenly, Uncle came swooshingly out of his bottle, more glowy and horrible than before.

He did his Hollow Laffs and his Terrible
Screams, then some new Terrible Words:

**SNIFF SNUFF SNARE, I SMELL BEAR!!
SNIFF SNUFF SNUP, I WILL EAT HIM UP!!**

Normus first got quiet. But then he said,
"Ghosts can't scare me! I'm a big bear! I like
shocks!"

So Uncle went, **"RRRRRAAAAARRRR!"**
And he did his Forest Fire and his Pack of
Hounds and his Swarm of Killer Bees.

But Normus just said, "Can't scare me! I can be nasty too—just look!" And he gave 3 hard kicks: 1 to me, 1 to Yeller, 1 to Stubbs. Then he sat on us, very hardly.

Uncle said, **"HOO HAR HAR, I KNEW IT! HE'S BLINKING BLUNKING TERRIFIED OF ME."**

But he wasn't really.

Yours squashedly,

Little

HAUNTED HALL SCHOOL

FRETTNIN FOREST, BEASTSHIRE
HEADS: LITTLE WOLF AND YELLER WOLF ESQS
DEPUTY HEAD: SMELLYBREFF WOLF ESQ
CARETAKER: STUBBS CROW ARKSQWIRE

Dear Mom and Dad,

What a big cheater Uncle is! I wrote a message on the back of a stamp and put it in his bottle for him to read. It said:

Hmm hmm, Uncle, you have lost your bet. Normus is not scared of you 1 bit. Now you must teach us your power of finding lost gold, etc.

Then out came his ghosty voice saying,

"GRRRRAAAAH! LAST NIGHT DOES NOT COUNT, I WAS NOT EVEN TRYING TO BE A TERROR, BUT JUST YOU WAIT! TONIGHT I SHALL SCARE THE BEAR'S FUR OFF!!"

Oh, boo. I forgot Rule of Badness number 9: NEVER trust a big bad wolf.

Yours cheatedly,
Silly me

HAUNTED HALL SCHOOL

FRETTNIN FOREST, BEASTSHIRE
HEADS: LITTLE WOLF AND YELLER WOLF ESQS
DEPUTY HEAD: SMELLYBREFF WOLF ESQ
CARETAKER: STUBBS CROW ARKSQWIRE

Dear Mom and Dad,

Ooo-er, Uncle was so scary in the night!
He did The Crawling Paw. He made the
paw go creepingly up the wall by itself
outside the dorm window. Then it went
scritch scratch with its nails. It made me call
out, "Ooo-er, help! Where are you, Stubbs
and Yeller?" But I didn't need to ask, because
all of a suddenly they were tucked up tight
right next to me!

Then I said, "Where is Normus?" Answer: fast
asleep. Not 1 bit nervous, even. But then he
had to get up to go to the lav. The dark was
deep, and the floorboards did *ee-arrs*. We held

our breaths waiting for a big shock. Then Normus pulled the chain and we heard: "SSSSHHHHHHHAAAAAAAH"!

Har, har! That was Uncle jumping out of the toilet, being a Terror!

But Normus just went back to bed yawningly. He did not even bother to light a candle. And before he got back in bed, he went *donk* on our heads with the toilet brush saying, "That's for you, becuz I hate your toilet. But toilets can't scare me, so there!"

Yours lumply,
Little

HAUNTED HALL SCHOOL

FRETTNIN FOREST, BEASTSHIRE
HEADS: LITTLE WOLF AND YELLER WOLF ESQS
DEPUTY HEAD: SMELLYBREFF WOLF ESQ
CARETAKER: STUBBS CROW ARKSQWIRE

Dear Mom and Dad,

Hope you can read this, because I am see-through (Yeller and Stubbs 2!) and maybe my ink is also! Shall I tell you how? Answer: by Uncle's training in secret powers!

Uncle has really got his temper up now. I was having a small zizz on the Ping-Pong table. It was still daytime and not nearly Uncle's haunting hours. But he broke the ghost rule and came out of his bottle to give me a message. He was 2 cross 2 stand still, so he dressed up as a Ping-Pong ball and used me as a net. He said:

Now I will tell you about Uncle's training. It's easy cheesy! All you do is hold on to a ghost's tail. Then his powers run through you, all tickly, and you can stay see-through till the 1st cocka-doodle of the dawn.

You can go *1-2-3 Pop!* And off comes your head. Or you can do a little hop and up you go floatingly like a small cloud. Hmm, nice feeling!

So in the deep dark, Uncle whispered, "FOLLOW ME." Up we went floatingly through the ceiling of the dorm going, "WOO!" We went through all the furniture, etc., plus we made all Normus's bedclothes go walking around him. And our best thing was turning into small skeletons, because then we got inside the cookie tin by Normus's bed and did a very noisy tap dance. Har, har!

Normus jumped out of bed, but not because of terror, oh no. He said, "Spooks and skellingtons can't scare me. I am tuff. I am ruff. Now I am going outside to bash up Smellybreff!"

What can we do to stop him?

Yours triedeverythingly,

L. Wolf

P.S. Uncle is no help. He just says "TUFF." Sorry.

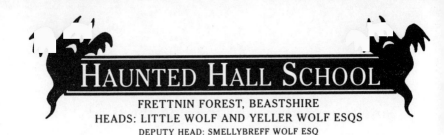

HAUNTED HALL SCHOOL

FRETTNIN FOREST, BEASTSHIRE
HEADS: LITTLE WOLF AND YELLER WOLF ESQS
DEPUTY HEAD: SMELLYBREFF WOLF ESQ
CARETAKER: STUBBS CROW ARKSQWIRE

Dear Mom and Dad,

Did you think to yourself: Hmmm, I was wondering Y Smells took that shovel when he ran off? Me 2. Answer: He went to his tent with it for digging a bear trap! So he did not get bashed after all—arrroooo!

We all peeped over the edge, and we saw Normus was down there, nice and deep. He saw us peeping and said, "Traps can't scare me. I will get out any minute, then I will bite you hard."

Yeller said, "TRUE. PLUS HE WILL SQUASH US AGAIN, I BET. QUICK, LET'S GET ALL STRICT!"

111

Stubbs said, "Ark! Wark!" meaning, yes, he is so arkward he deserves a hard whack. Also Smells wanted to donk him on the head with his shovel.

But I said, "No, no more bashing!"

Yeller said, "BUT Y NOT? HE IS A BIG BULLY! HE BASHED US AND SQUASHED US, AND NOW IT'S OUR TURN. REMEMBER THE SAYING: IF YOU GET BASHED, BASH BACK HARDER!"

I said, "But everybody bashes Normus. It doesn't do any good. His mom bashes him. His dad bashes him. Even his sister bashes him."

Stubbs said, "Ark! Shark!" meaning he needs a short, sharp shock, because he pulled out my best feathers!

I said, "No more bashing, no more shocks, no more strictness. This is what we'll do." I did an important whisper to all of them and off they went thinkingly to work.

Then I said down the bear trap, "Normus, are you listening? We are going to fetch a ladder to let you up."

Normus just said, "Good, becuz then I can squash your heads in."

Yours ooo-erly,
Little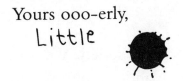

HAUNTED HALL SCHOOL

FRETTNIN FOREST, BEASTSHIRE
HEADS: LITTLE WOLF AND YELLER WOLF ESQS
DEPUTY HEAD: SMELLYBREFF WOLF ESQ
CARETAKER: STUBBS CROW ARKSQWIRE

Dear Mom and Dad,

Da-daaah! Just in case you thought, oh no, our boy is killed dead by a head squash, here I am again.

Because listen what happened. We got ready, then we put the ladder down the trap. Normus started climbing up going *grrr* and *grufff.* I said, "Normus, have you ever had a chum?"

He said, "What's a chum?"

I said, "You know, a friend, or somebody that likes you and only does pretend bites."

Normus said, "No, I haven't got 1. Everybody hates me."

Then he read:

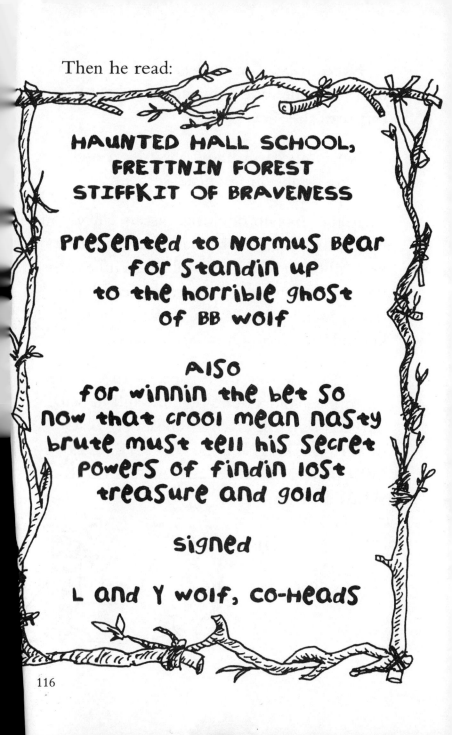

HAUNTED HALL SCHOOL,
FRETTNIN FOREST
STIFFKIT OF BRAVENESS

Presented to Normus Bear
for standin up
to the horrible ghost
of BB wolf

AlSO
for winnin the bet So
now that crool mean nasty
brute must tell his secret
powers of findin lost
treasure and gold

signed

L and Y wolf, co-Heads

I said, "Aha! But that was before. This is after. So come out now and have your surprise."

Normus said, "I know about surprises— they are donks on my head!"

I said, "No, no donking! Listen, I like you, Yeller likes you, Stubbs likes you. You have won a bet, and now we will be rich because you are the only brute beast in Beastshire with the braveness to stand up to Uncle Bigbad."

Yeller held out a stiff paper with writing on in nice colors done by him, and he said, "NORMUS BEAR, I PRESENT YOU WITH A STIFFKIT OF BRAVENESS. WELL DONE. AND BECAUSE YOUR READING IS NO GOOD, I WILL SAY THE WORDS FOR YOU."

Normus said, "You mean you really like me? Even the crow? Even that small diggy cub with the shovel?"

I said, "Well, not Smells, no. He hates everybody. But the rest of us."

A big tear fell off Normus's nose and he said, "This is the best, most scaryest school I know. I'm not going  home. Ever. I want to stay and have chums."

And we said all right then, you can be our 1st proper pupil. Then Stubbs flew up to the bell tower and gave the bell a hard *ding* for Haunted Hall's 1st proper daytime lesson: Spooksuit Making.

Yours proudly,
L. Wolf Esqwire
(Co-Head)

HAUNTED HALL SCHOOL

FRETTNIN FOREST, BEASTSHIRE
HEADS: LITTLE WOLF AND YELLER WOLF ESQS
DEPUTY HEAD: SMELLYBREFF WOLF ESQ
CARETAKER: STUBBS CROW ARKSQWIRE

Normal Boring School

Dear Mom and Dad,

Big shock! We took Normus into the pantry to meet Uncle in his bottle, and to say, "Come on, be a sport, pay up your bet." But, oh no! A burglar has been there stealing things! It was while we were all in the back garden. And guess what he ~~burglard~~ ~~stealed~~ ~~burguled~~ stole? Answer: the bottle!

Oh, boo! Now we will never find out the power of finding lost treasure, and that is the end of Haunted Hall. Because the burglar has got the "haunted" part—in other words, Uncle! Boo, shame. Now Normus will probly think we are now just a normal boring school and go home.

Yours startagainly,

L.

118

Dear Mom and Dad,

Thank you for your LOUD LETTER about the shame of losing our best relative. You ask will he ever Moan in Peace again? Also you say I have let down the name of the pack, so Dad has gone all sulky. He says he will not come and visit us here ever, not till his lost bro is back in his happy haunting ground.

OK. I will try my hardest to go hunting for that burglar. Off I trot.

Yours scentingly,
    Little the tracker

Dear Mom and Dad,

All I have found so far is 1 will-of-the-whisker at the marshy end of the forest and some tracks, but sad to say made by skunks, not Uncle. Yeller came and found me. He has not found Uncle either. He says Smells is all upset. He took the stuffing out of his ted to look in it, in case Uncle was hiding in there, but no luck. Now, just because he put the stuffing back wrong, he says Yeller stole his ted and left behind a fat tortoise.

Stubbs says he will help restuff Smell's ted properly, but not just yet. When he was highflying and looking down owlholes, he bonked into a branch. So a sore beak for Stubbs too. Boo, shame. Plus Normus got his head wedged in a can of peaches. Maybe he thought Uncle wanted a bath in peach juice.

Will we ever find Uncle's trail?

Yours lipnibblingly,

Little

Wolf Hall (not haunted at moment)

Dear Mom and Dad,

As I said, no luck yesterday, but today everybody went around the house looking for clues with magnifying glasses and notebooks and sharp pencils. We got very tired and fedup, but by snacktime, everybody had found maybe 1 small cluelet:

Smells found 1 foxy pawprint (found in rosebed outside pantry window).

Normus found 2 red whiskers.

Stubbs found 1 button from a Ranger's jacket.

Yeller found 1 nose smudge on a custard in the pantry.

And I found 1 Ranger's hat that made me sneezy.

Add them all up and they = 1 greedy
Ranger with red whiskers and a smell like
pepper who knows about Uncle Bigbad's
power of finding lost treasure.

I said, "Hmm, let me think. That
is just like the Mountain Ranger
who let me get captured by
Normus's dad! He was peppery.
I also noticed his coat was bulgy

at the back. Ooo-er! Now I know who that
was! He was not a Ranger at all. He was
that Wanted crook and Master of Dizgizzes
(cannot spell it), MISTER TWISTER!"

Yours,

Sherlock Wolf (get it?)

HAUNTED HALL SCHOOL

FRETTNIN FOREST, BEASTSHIRE
HEADS: LITTLE WOLF AND YELLER WOLF ESQS
DEPUTY HEAD: SMELLYBREFF WOLF ESQ
CARETAKER: STUBBS CROW ARKSQWIRE

The Yelloweyes Forest Detective Agency

Dear Mom and Dad,

Normus says clue hunts are his best game ever and never mind about Haunted Hall closing, but can he be in our pack? He likes being our chum, but he also wants to be a detective. Good, huh?

So from now on we are all going to do solving crimes and mysteries all over the forest. No more schools, no more horrors, no more Haunted Hall.

We are The Yelloweyes Forest Detectives!

124

So look out, all you big robbers and crooks like Mister Twister! The YFDA is on your trail!

Yours elementary-my-dear-mom-and-dadly,

L. Wolf, Forest Detective

[French]